P9-DXD-427

A Night on the Town

Caroline Merola

Tundra Books

Originally published as *Une nuit en ville* by Editions Les 400 coups, 2007
Text and illustrations copyright © 2007 by Caroline Merola

First English translation published in Canada by Tundra Books, 2010
75 Sherbourne Street, Toronto, Ontario M5A 2P9

First published in Canada in 2007 by les editions Les 400 coups

Published in the United States by Tundra Books of Northern New York,
P.O. Box 1030, Plattsburgh, New York 12901

Library of Congress Control Number: 2009938454

Library and Archives Canada Cataloguing in Publication

Merola, Caroline
[Nuit en ville. English]
      A night on the town / Caroline Merola.

Translation of: Une nuit en ville.
ISBN 978-1-77049-200-4

      I. Title.

PS8576.E7358N8513 2009   jC843'.54   C2009-905948-7

We acknowledge the financial support of the Government of Canada through the Book
Publishing Industry Development Program (BPIDP) and that of the Government of
Ontario through the Ontario Media Development Corporation's Ontario Book Initiative.
We further acknowledge the support of the Canada Council for the Arts and the Ontario
Arts Council for our publishing program.

ONTARIO ARTS COUNCIL
CONSEIL DES ARTS DE L'ONTARIO

Printed and bound in China

1 2 3 4 5 6   15 14 13 12 11 10

For Robert and Colombe,
my precious friends

Pickles McPhee had longed for adventure, so when the chance came along for a ride into town, she took it. She'd never been to town before, but she suspected she'd find adventure there.

She was amazed by the towering buildings, the smooth paved roads, and especially the lights that shone everywhere. She wandered up one street and down another. And then, she noticed Martha.

Martha sat by the window, trying to stay awake. She was expecting the tooth fairy. The sight of Pickles McPhee surprised her. "Wow, the tooth fairy is so big and has horns and blue stripes!"

Pickles had never heard of a tooth fairy, but she was quite certain that she wasn't one. "I'm Pickles McPhee," she said, "and I'm looking for an adventure. Do you know where I could find one?"

To tell the truth, Martha had grown
tired of waiting for the tooth fairy. And
though she lived in town, she had rarely
seen it by night. She knew many rules,
but not the rule about what to do if a blue,
striped, horned creature with a sweet smile
appeared in the middle of the night. She was
as ready for adventure as anyone. She took
Pickles' blue paw in her hand and climbed out
the window. "Let's go!" she said. "There's bound
to be an adventure in the park."

Everything looked and sounded different at night. The park, where Martha played every day, seemed like a strange, new land. Pickles climbed a tree and let Martha swing from her paws. They laughed until their sides ached.

The pool was closed, of course, but that didn't stop Pickles. She loved the water. She swam up and down with Martha on her back. "Yippee! I'm riding a sea horse!" cried Martha.

All this adventure was making both of them
hungry. The restaurants were long closed,
but Martha had an idea.

"There's a candy store just up the street."
She held out her arms to Pickles. "Up, please.
If you carry me, we'll get there sooner,"
she said.

The candy store was shut tight. Pickles rattled the doorknob again and again.

"Try harder! There are caramels and lollipops inside. Every color you can imagine." Martha was growing tired and hungry and cranky. "Open the door, or I won't play with you anymore!"

That was a rather mean thing to say, and Pickles didn't want the adventure to end unhappily. With a swing of her tail she broke the door. Martha pushed past and dove into a bucket of candy.

Pickles had never tasted candy before. She tried a lollipop. "Not bad," she said. "Not bad at all. This is fun!"

The fun didn't last long.
You can't smash a door in
the middle of the night, even if
there's candy on the other side.
Before Pickles and Martha knew
it, two big policemen with dogs
appeared. Martha ducked behind
the candy counter, but there was
no place big enough for Pickles to
hide.

"What in the world is *that*?"
cried one policeman.

"It's a savage beast! It's
a wild monster! It's about to
attack!" shouted the other
officer.

Pickles wasn't a savage beast
or a wild monster, and she wasn't
about to attack. But she was very
frightened.

Pickles looked around for Martha but couldn't see her. There was only one thing to do. *Run!* Pickles charged outside and fled down the street, past the swimming pool, and into the park. The park had been so inviting when she'd been there with Martha, but now it was menacing and scary.

Terrified and alone, Pickles finally had to stop. She was out of breath. This was not the adventure she'd wanted.

The policemen caught up in no time. "Aha, we've got the monster cornered!" they shouted. They were just reaching for their handcuffs when a little shadow appeared, followed by Martha.

Martha had been running behind, hoping to sneak home before anyone realized she was missing. When she saw poor, terrified Pickles, she was ashamed of herself.

"Don't you touch her! Pickles is *not* a monster," explained Martha. "She's *my friend*."

The police listened carefully, while Martha
told them the truth and nothing but the truth
about their adventurous night on the town.
When she was finished, the officers decided to
walk Martha home. She took Pickles by the
paw, and they all set out.

Naturally, Martha's parents were a little
confused when they answered the door. After
many questions and explanations, the police
finally left.

Martha knew that her parents were angry with her for breaking so many rules.

"I was wrong to go out at night," she admitted, "and I was double-wrong to talk to a stranger – even if I thought she was the tooth fairy at first." Martha turned to Pickles. "And I was wrong to be mean and to hide when the police came. I'm very sorry."

Everyone saw how truly sorry she was. And they saw how tired she was. "It's time for bed," said her mother. "Pickles, you may sleep here tonight. In the morning, we'll take you home."

The next day, they piled into the car and headed to the heart of the forest. The McPhees were very thankful to see their daughter. "Pickles, let's have no more adventuring!" Pickles thought about how frightened she'd been, and she agreed. But when she and Martha said good-bye, she knew that laughing with her best friend until her sides ached on a warm summer night had been worth it all.